Mr Bear
to the Rescue

Debi Gliori

ORCHARD BOOKS

For all of those Mr Bears:
Guri and Kari, Gay and Michael,
Ben, Sophie and Patrick,
my very dear Kirsty,
Belinda and Lyndsay
Jaca and Judy
but most of all
for you.
You.

ORCHARD BOOKS
96 Leonard Street
London EC2A 4XD
Orchard Books Australia
Unit 31/56 O'Riordan Street, Alexandria, NSW 2015
ISBN 1 84121 768 9
First published in Great Britain in 1996
This edition published in 2001
Copyright © Debi Gliori 2001
The right of Debi Gliori to be identified as the author and
illustrator of this work has been asserted by her in accordance
with the Copyright, Designs and Patents Act, 1988.
A CIP catalogue record for this book is available from the British Library.
10 9 8 7 6 5 4 3
Printed in Hong Kong/China

It was a wild and windy night in the forest.

The kind of night where the best place to be
was indoors, snug and warm, with windows
and doors tightly shut to keep the weather out.

Mr Bear was tucked up
in bed listening to the wind
howling outside.

"Do you hear that?"
said Mrs Bear. "It sounds like
someone calling *Help!*"

"It's just the wind, dear,"
said Mr Bear.

"Help!" said a small voice.

"There," said Mrs Bear,
"I *did* hear someone. Go and
see who it is, dear?"

Mr Bear went downstairs and
opened the front door.

"Please help," said a very small
voice from somewhere around
Mr Bear's ankles.

Clinging onto the doorstep
was Mr Rabbit-Bunn.

"Our warren has collapsed,"
he wailed. "The Hoot-Toowits' nest
has blown away, the Buzzes' hive is
ruined and we can't find baby Flora
anywhere," and Mr Rabbit-Bunn
vanished into the night.

"Help is on its way," said Mr Bear, grabbing
tools and a honey sandwich, just in case.

"Do be careful, dear," called Mrs Bear.

"Don't worry," said Mr Bear, as he blew
down the garden. "I'll be fine."

It was a long way to the Rabbit-Bunns' house.
Mr Bear tripped and stumbled over fallen branches
and several times his lantern nearly blew out.

"Aaaaargh!" shrieked Mr Bear as a tangle of
feathers and claws blew into his face.
"Eeeek!" squawked Mr Hoot-Toowit.
"Oh, it's *you*!" they both
cried in unison.

"I can't see your house anywhere,"
said Mr Bear, peering into the darkness.
"You're standing in it," said Mr Hoot-Toowit sadly.
There lay the remains of the tree that the Hoot-Toowits
had shared with the Buzzes and the Rabbit-Bunns.

"Oh Mr Bear, thank heavens you've come,"
cried a voice. "Can you help us find Flora?"
"And can you fix our hive?"
"And mend our nest?"

Mr Bear found himself surrounded by
rabbits and owls and bees.
"Help," thought Mr Bear. "What on earth
am I supposed to do?"
He scrabbled around in his toolkit and
found his honey sandwich.
A brilliant idea suddenly occurred to him.

"What's that for?" asked one of the small
Rabbit-Bunns.

"Glue," said Mr Bear, peeling the sandwich
apart. "Hive-glue, in fact. Look, I'll spread a little
bit here and another dollop there and…"

"End up with a sticky mess," groaned a small Buzz.
"Oh dear," said Mr Bear. "Mrs Bear will fix that.
She's very good at that sort of thing."

"What about my nest?" said Mr Hoot-Toowit.
"Let's see," said Mr Bear, picking it up.

The nest fell apart in his paws. Mrs Hoot-Toowit sighed.
"Um, yes," said Mr Bear. "Mrs Bear'll knit you
another in no time."

The animals put the sticky hive and broken nest
into Mr Bear's toolkit, just as the heavens opened.

Rain poured down through the trees,
and the animals ran for shelter.

Mr Bear's lantern hissed, fizzled and went out.

"How will we ever find Flora now?" wailed Mrs Rabbit-Bunn.

Mr Bear anxiously looked up at the sky.

"Good grief," he cried. "I've found her!"
There, high in the branches of the sheltering
tree, was a tiny rabbit, wrapped in her blanket
and fast asleep.

"I'll just climb up and get her,"
said Mr Bear.

"What a hero you are," sighed
Mrs Rabbit-Bunn.

But Mr Bear didn't feel heroic
as he inched up the slippery tree,
which creaked and groaned with
every move.

At last he disentangled the blanket,
cradled Flora in his arms and...

"Aaaaargh!" yelled Mr Bear.
"Wheeeeeee!" said Flora, waking up.
"Gosh, what a good idea,"
said Mr Rabbit-Bunn as
Flora's blanket fanned out
into a perfect parachute…

...and Mr Bear and the bunny
floated safely to the ground.

"What a brilliant Mr Bear!" said
Mrs Rabbit-Bunn, hugging Mr Bear's knees.
Mr Bear relit his lantern and loaded all
his friends into his toolkit.
"Hold tight!" he said. "I'm taking you home."

Back through the storm they went till they reached the top of the hill and could see Mr Bear's house in the distance with its lights on.

"Not far now," he said. "We're nearly there."

Mrs Bear had been busy organising beds for everyone and, much later, when her hot nettle soup had warmed every tummy, large and small, the Bear house filled with snores.

Then Mr Bear sank into a chair with a groan.
Baby Bear clambered onto his tummy.
"What a brilliant Mr Bear your Daddy is,"
said Mrs Bear. "So good at fixing things."
Mr Bear gave a huge yawn.

"In fact," continued Mrs Bear,
"I have some more things for that Daddy to fix.
There's the squeaky bathroom door, the blocked
sink and the smoky chimney…"
Mr Bear gave a loud snore.

"…but they can all wait until tomorrow," said Mrs Bear.
"Even brilliant Mr Bears need a bit of rescuing at times,"
she said, tucking a blanket around Mr Bear and the
baby and heading upstairs to bed.